The

OT

Charlie Chameleon:

New Beginnings

written by
Ellen L. Buikema

illustrated by
Elizabeth Engel

Running Horse Press

Sun City West, AZ

For information, contact:
Running Horse Press
www.runninghorsepress.com
14819 W. Yosemite Drive
Sun City West, AZ 85375

Cover design and illustrations by Elizabeth Engel
Book design and typesetting by Gale Leach

Published by Running Horse Press

ISBN: 978-0-9908979-3-4
LCCN: 2015918805

For information about special discounts for bulk purchases, please contact Running Horse Press at 575-650-2246 or info@runninghorsepress.com.

To Ralph
who listened, read, and laughed
in the right places.

Acknowledgements

I am grateful for the help I've received from family, friends, and members of the West Valley Writer's and Northwest Valley Writer's critique groups.

A special thank you to Ami Montoya who was involved in the early stages of the Charlie stories.

Contents

The Adventures of Charlie Chameleon:

New Beginnings

Our New Home

Charlie Chameleon sat up in bed. His tail was wrapped around his blanket. Charlie looked at his pet fish swimming in the aquarium. "Frankie, it's time for breakfast."

Frankie swam to the top of the tank. "Yummy. Do I get Sugar Buggies?"

"I don't know, Frankie. Sugar Buggies make you hyper."

"Pleeeease, just a few?"

"Oh, okay. I guess it won't hurt. Let's go downstairs, Frankie."

Frankie swam in circles, jumped into the air, and landed with a splash in his fishbowl, right next to his aquarium.

Charlie walked downstairs cradling Frankie, safe in the fishbowl, by his arm. Frankie went everywhere with Charlie.

Papa Chameleon sat at the kitchen table, drinking coffee as he read his newspaper. "Good morning, Charlie. Mama made us a wonderful breakfast." Papa gave Mama a big smile.

"Charlie, put Frankie down and eat your waxworm cereal while it's still warm," said Mama.

Frankie blew bubbles out of his fishbowl. One bubble landed on Charlie's breakfast. Another bubble popped on Charlie's nose. "Yuck. Fish breath. Frankie, stop blowing bubbles. Here, have some Sugar Buggies."

Papa got up from the table and gave Mama and Charlie a hug. He whistled to himself as he got ready to go to work. Papa had great news

and wanted to tell his family, but he was not sure how Mama and Charlie would feel.

Just before dinner, Charlie sat at the kitchen table, coloring a spaceship in his new activity book.

Frankie poked his head out of the fish bowl. "Charlie, let me help you. There's not enough color." Frankie spat water on Charlie's page. The book was soaked.

"Frankie, the water didn't help. It just messed up my book. I should bring you upstairs, so you can't wreck my stuff." Charlie stood up and was about to take Frankie upstairs when he heard Papa come in the front door.

"Mama, Charlie, I have good news! Come sit with me in the living room," Papa called out to them. Mama sat down in her favorite chair, the pink one with large flowers on it. Charlie ran over to the couch and bounced up and down with Frankie's fishbowl in his arms.

Frankie's face turned green. "I'm getting seasick. S … T … O … P."

"Charlie, be careful! You'll fall off and hurt yourself!" said Mama.

"Sorry, Mama," said Charlie, wiggling on the couch. Charlie looked out the window, hoping to go outside and play with his friends. Tamika Turtle, Charlie's best friend, was across the street playing with a soccer ball.

Papa walked back and forth in front of Mama and Charlie. "I have a new job. It will be in the same town where Grandma and Grandpa Chameleon live. Isn't that great?"

Charlie's head whipped away from the window. "Papa, when you take the new job, will you still have time to play soccer with me?" he asked. "I don't know anyone in New Town."

"You don't have to worry about anything. We'll move soon. You'll have time to meet new friends before starting school, Charlie," said Papa. "Here are some pictures of our new home. It comes with the job."

"It's beautiful! There are enough rooms to have friends stay with us. Oh, the kitchen is huge," said Mama Chameleon, hugging Papa. Charlie could see that his mom and dad were happy about this change. He wasn't sure how he felt.

Charlie was very quiet. He looked out the window at his friend, Tamika, and rocked back and forth, hugging Frankie's bowl. Tears formed in his eyes. Charlie looked down and saw Frankie crying in his fishbowl.

Charlie whispered, "Papa, I don't want to move. My friends are here. My school is here. My soccer team is here."

Papa sat down on the couch next to Charlie. "I know you feel sad about moving. Let's talk about what we can do," said Papa, putting his arm around Charlie.

"I promised my friend, Tamika, that we would try out for the same soccer team. Now I won't be able to practice with her," said Charlie still looking down. "I don't want to leave my friends!"

Papa wiped away Charlie's tears.

"I know you love to play soccer, Charlie. When we move we'll live closer to my job, so I'll have more time to practice with you. We can invite Tamika over so you can still play together. I hear there is a traveling soccer team that both of you can join."

"Really?" sniffed Charlie looking at Papa. "We could still play together?"

"Yes, and your other friends can come, too! If you want to be on the traveling team it will take a lot of practice. What do you say, Charlie?" Papa asked.

Charlie grinned. "I say yes!" He put Frankie's bowl on the coffee table. "Sorry, Frankie, I need to tell Tamika!" Charlie yelled, as he rushed outside to see his best friend.

Charlie crossed the street to Tamika Turtle's house. She was practicing soccer in the Turtle family's front yard. He couldn't wait to tell her the news.

Tamika kicked her soccer ball into the net. "I shot and a score. WHOO-HOO, I am a soccer hero!" Tamika Turtle ran in a circle, arms up in the air.

"Tamika, nice shot. You're good. Almost as good as I am!" said Charlie, laughing.

"Right, Charlie, but I can run faster than you." Tamika kicked the ball back and forth with Charlie.

"Maybe, but I can kick the ball better." Charlie moved the soccer ball away from Tamika and kicked the ball into the net. "I am the soccer king!" Charlie shouted loud enough for Tamika's mom to hear from inside the house.

Charlie thought Mrs. Turtle was different. She wore a headband every day, and exercised all the time. She made lots of weird food she said was good for you, but it tasted funny. He liked the stuff his mom cooked better.

"Tamika, Charlie, come in. I just finished making some smoothies. I know you'll love them!" said Mrs. Turtle. "You know, both of you are getting bigger every day."

"Aww, Mom, you always say that," said Tamika winking at Charlie. "Did you put berries in it this time? Last time you used snails and it made me pucker. Berries are better."

"Yes, I did use berries. You are in luck. Enjoy your smoothies," said Mrs. Turtle. "I have to do my exercises. Today, I'm doing Zumba with Ashley. Please clean up after yourselves."

"Your Mom is so nice! It will be weird not walking across the street to visit you and having one of your Mom's smoothies," said Charlie, looking into his empty glass.

"What do you mean, not coming across the street? Charlie, what's wrong?" Tamika put her hand on Charlie's shoulder and tried to look him in the eye.

Charlie looked away. He didn't want Tamika to see him sad. "Papa has a new job near Grandma and Grandpa. We're moving. I'll be at a different school."

"What! No, you are my best friend, Charlie. You can't move away. You can stay here with my mom and me. She'll say it's okay," shouted Tamika.

"What is all that noise, children? I'm trying to exercise," said Mrs. Turtle, walking into the room.

"Mom, Charlie's Mama and Papa have to move. Charlie can live here with us, right?" asked Tamika.

Mrs. Turtle put her hand on Tamika's back. With a heavy sigh, she said, "No honey, Charlie needs to live with his family. If he stayed here with us his Mama and Papa would be very sad. They would worry about him all the time." Turning to Charlie, she said, "Charlie, we will miss you. Any time you want to visit, call, okay?"

"Thank you, Mrs. Turtle," sniffed Charlie. Mrs. Turtle hugged Charlie and Tamika then walked back to her room.

"I have to get back home, Tamika. Tell your Mom the smoothie was delicious." Charlie handed Tamika a piece of paper with his new email address on it.

"What's this for?" Tamika asked.

"It's my email address. My mom says we can be pen pals," said Charlie.

"Pen pals? What's that?"

"Pen pals are friends that write letters to each other, except we'll be email pals, no pens needed."

"We'll always be friends!" Tamika gave Charlie a quick hug.

"Right! We can write email in secret code."

Tamika and Charlie walked to her front door. "My papa said there is a traveling soccer team. Maybe we can both play on it," said Charlie. "Do you want to practice making goals tomorrow?"

"Sure, Charlie! See you tomorrow." From her front door Tamika Turtle watched Charlie walk home.

Charlie felt better. He knew even though he was moving away, Tamika would still be his friend. He was excited about having an email pal, using secret code. He couldn't wait to tell Frankie all about his plans.

Mrs. Turtle's Berry Smoothie
(makes one serving)

Use one peeled banana, one cup fresh or frozen berries, and one-half cup water or milk. Blend with a blender. (Make sure the top is on!) Pour in a glass. Serve with a straw and enjoy!

Moving Day

Charlie Chameleon looked around his room, deciding how to pack. There were so many toys! Behind him, Frankie leapt, splashing in and out of the aquarium next to the bedroom wall.

"Frankie, it's hard for me to think with all that noise. I can't decide what to pack first."

Charlie sat on the floor hidden from Frankie's view. He picked up a toy to pack in a box.

"I can't see you, Charlie. I need to see what you're doing so I can help," said Frankie from his fish tank.

"Oh, all right, Frankie. Let me fit this water-helmet on you. Then you can come closer and see what I'm doing."

Charlie dipped the helmet into Frankie's tank, and put him into the helmet just past his gills. Charlie closed the seal and flipped Frankie onto his strong tail fins so Frankie could watch him from the bed. Frankie bent his head down to see what Charlie was doing.

"Well, pick one corner of the room to pack at a time. Then, choose the next corner. The toys will be packed in a flash," said Frankie from the top of Charlie's bed.

"Thanks, Frankie! You have great ideas." Charlie moved closer to Frankie.

"Wait." Frankie looked worried. "Don't hug me. You know I don't like being squished!"

Charlie stopped and put his arms down.

"Oh, that's right. No hugs for fish. Sorry."

Charlie's mom yelled up the stairs, "Charlie! We can't move until you finish packing your toys!"

"I'm almost done."

"Whee!" Frankie jumped up and down on Charlie's bed.

"Stop that jumping, Frankie. Water might leak from your helmet. Then you won't have enough left in the helmet to breathe!" said Charlie.

"What was that about jumping on the bed?" asked Mama from the stairway.

"Nothing, Mama, it's just Frankie being silly."

19

Charlie pushed the last boxes out of his room so Mama and Papa could carry them down the stairs and into the moving van. Frankie, balanced on top of the last box, waved a tiny toy sword in one fin.

"Forward ho! Off we go. We are on our way, with new places to play," sang Frankie at the top of his gills.

"Frankie, you're a poet and you don't know it," laughed Charlie.

Mama sat in the moving van holding Frankie's tank on her lap. She waited calmly for Papa and Charlie to get in the van.

Tamika Turtle ran out of her house and waved goodbye to her best friend.

"Goodbye, Tamika," said Charlie trying not to be sad.

"Charlie, I'll see you real soon." Tamika smiled and waved as the van drove off.

Three hours later, the truck pulled up to the Chameleon family's new home. Each house on the block looked a little different.

"Wow. Papa, I didn't know our new house was so big."

"Look, Frankie!" said Charlie. "Our house is covered in rocks and the front door is round."

"Thank goodness it's a round door. It will be easy to get all the furniture inside." Papa got out of the van and started to unload it.

"Charlie, why don't you take Frankie inside," said Mama. "I'll be right in."

"Come on, Frankie! Let's go to our new room!" Charlie and Frankie shouted as they ran inside the house and up the stairs. Charlie bumped into a stack of boxes. The top box fell on the floor.

CRASH.

"Charlie!" yelled Mama as she walked into the house.

"Sorry!" Charlie said, while Frankie moved back and forth with the water in his fishbowl.

Charlie and Frankie looked around their new room. "This is so cool! We can make it the best room ever."

"Yep," agreed Frankie. "How?"

"I don't know," said Charlie as they sat on the floor together, looking around the empty room.

Later that evening, as they ate earthworm spaghetti for dinner, Mama asked, "Charlie, what do you think of our new home?"

Charlie looked down at his plate and moved a cricket meatball around the maze of noodles. "I already miss my friends." Tears formed in his eyes.

Mama heard Frankie slurping spaghetti from Papa's plate while he wasn't looking. "Frankie, stop that or no more meals with the family."

Frankie dropped the noodle and sank to the bottom of his fishbowl.

"Charlie, I know you will make new friends," Mama said.

"I sure hope so . . . ." He pushed the noodles around on his plate, not feeling very hungry.

"I'll eat it!" said Frankie. "Give me cheese, lots of cheese."

"Sure." Charlie got up from the table and asked to be excused. He climbed the stairs to his room, feeling sad about leaving his old home.

Papa carried the spaghetti-filled Frankie up to Charlie's room. He found Charlie putting his toys away on a shelf. "Are you okay, Charlie?"

"Yeah," Charlie replied sadly. "I just miss my old home and friends."

Papa set Frankie's fishbowl down on Charlie's dresser next to the aquarium. Then he put his arms around Charlie and gave him a hug. "Mama and I agree. You'll make many friends." Papa looked around Charlie's room. "You put away a lot of toys, Charlie. You're tired and that is making you feel worse. It's time to get ready for bed. Mama will stop in later."

"Okay, Papa."

Frankie swam in lazy circles and poked his head out of the fishbowl. "BURP."

"Frankie, no more spaghetti for you."

"Charlie," yawned Frankie, "I need my beauty sleep." Frankie jumped from his fishbowl into the aquarium to sleep for the night.

Charlie crawled into bed. "Goodnight, Frankie."

"Goodnight, Charlie."

Charlie turned off the light. He heard Frankie blowing bubbles as he snored in the aquarium. Soon, Charlie's eyes felt too heavy to keep open. All his troubles melted away as he drifted off to sleep.

The next morning Charlie opened his eyes and wondered where he was. Then he remembered. This was his new home. He looked across the room at the aquarium on top of the dresser. Frankie was still asleep. Charlie got up and brushed his teeth. He walked downstairs and sat at the table. He was a little more cheerful today.

"Good morning, Charlie." Mama poured milk over his Crispy Cricket Flakes cereal.

"Morning, Mama."

Papa mixed water into eggs in a pan. "The eggs will be done in a minute."

"Thank you, Papa."

"Charlie, after you finish breakfast, you should check your email. This morning Papa and I discovered we already have internet access. Maybe there's something in your email that will cheer you up.

"Really? That would be great news!"

Charlie finished his Crispy Cricket Flakes and scrambled eggs and excused himself to leave the table. He took a spoonful of scrambled eggs for Frankie. Upstairs, Charlie found Frankie swishing a toy sword with one fin.

"Take that . . . and that," he said, pointing the sword at a toy mermaid on a rock at the bottom of the aquarium.

"Hey, Frankie, let's check my email."

Charlie turned on his laptop, opened a browser, and then checked his email.

"What's in your email?" asked Frankie, peering through the glass wall of his tank.

"It's a message from Tamika!" Inside was a bunch of mixed up numbers and symbols. Charlie didn't understand what she wrote.

Then Charlie realized Tamika had written in code! "How will I ever know what the code is?"

DEAR CHARLIE,

   IF YOU ARE READING
THIS, THAT MEANS YOU
CRACKED THE CODE. I
HOPE YOU LIKE YOUR NEW
HOME. SOCCER WON'T BE
THE SAME WITHOUT YOU.
I HOPE YOU FIND NEW
FRIENDS AND A SOCCER
TEAM IN YOUR NEW TOWN.
I CAN'T WAIT TO GET A
LETTER BACK FROM YOU.
WRITE BACK TO ME USING
THE SAME CODE. I MISS
YOU!

         YOUR FRIEND,
           TAMIKA

He stared at the mystery letters. Then he remembered what Grandpa Chameleon told him about writing in codes. There's always a pattern.

What's the pattern? he thought.

Charlie tore a piece of paper from his notebook and started counting and writing the letters. "I did it! I've solved the code."

Charlie immediately wrote an email to Tamika, in code. The message she sent made him feel a lot better.

He looked at Frankie, who had been very quiet. Charlie smiled. Frankie was asleep in his aquarium near the tiny mermaid.

Charlie dashed downstairs and into the living room where Mama sat in her favorite comfy chair.

"Thank you, Mama. You were right. Tamika sent me a message in secret code. I sent an email back to her already. Oh, no! I forgot to send it!" Charlie yelled as he ran back upstairs.

CRASH!

"Charlie!" yelled Mama.

"Whoops, sorry." He walked back into his room, pressed send on his computer, and sat down on the bed. He was feeling much happier about his new home. Charlie knew he would still have his friend, Tamika, no matter what.

Just then Frankie woke up.

"Hey, Charlie, what did I miss?" yawned Frankie.

Charlie smiled and replied, "Nothing at all." Charlie knew everything was going to be okay.

Activity:

Can you decode Tamika's letter to Charlie?

A = 1	N = &
B = 2	O = ¢
C = 3	P = Ω
D = 4	Q = ¶
E = 5	R = ∞
F = 6	S = *
G = 7	T = ©
H = 8	U = ^
I = 9	V = ≠
J = @	W = ®
K = #	X = «
L = $	Y = Δ
M = %	Z = ~

A New Friend

SPLISH! SPLASH! SPLUNK! Charlie woke up to find Frankie jumping up and down in his fishbowl. Frankie flipped, splashing water on Charlie.

"Wake up, Charlie! Wake up!"

"I don't want to." Charlie grumbled and pulled his blue blanket over his head.

"WAKE UP!" Frankie shouted, soaking Charlie's blanket. "It's morning! Let's go explore our new neighborhood!"

Charlie groaned as he got up. He stomped downstairs, while holding Frankie's fishbowl.

Frankie's face turned green. "Stop stomping. I'm gonna slosh right out of my bowl."

"Sorry, Frankie. I guess I'm in a bad mood."

Charlie put Frankie's fishbowl on the kitchen table and plopped down on his chair, sighing.

Papa Chameleon sat at the table, his face hidden behind a newspaper. "Good morning, Charlie."

"Morning," Charlie grumbled back.

Mama Chameleon looked up from her tablet. "What's wrong, Charlie?"

"I don't think I'll make new friends here. I miss my old friends."

"You'll make friends. Take a chance. Talk to them," Papa chimed in from behind the newspaper.

"I guess," Charlie groaned.

Charlie poked at his cereal. "Mama, I'm not all that hungry."

Frankie raised his head out of his bowl. "Give me some. I want your cereal."

"Forget it, Frankie. The last time I gave you some of my Sugar Buggies you went hyper, and I was sorry."

"Charlie, eat more of your breakfast, and then you and Frankie can explore the neighborhood."

Charlie finished his breakfast, excused himself from the table, and got ready to go outside.

"Mom, do you know where Frankie's portable fish tank is? We're gonna go out and explore the new neighborhood."

"Sure. It's in the hallway closet, next to the vacuum cleaner."

"Okay, Mom. Come on, Frankie. It's time to fill up the tank."

Charlie grabbed the portable tank in one hand and cradled Frankie's fishbowl with the other arm as he walked to the kitchen sink.

Frankie swam furious circles, waiting to change locations. "Here I go. Geronimo!" Frankie leapt out of his fishbowl into the tank just as Charlie finished filling it.

"Frankie, I wish you'd let me scoop you into the tank. You scare me when you jump in."

"You scare me when you scoop. Fish don't like hugs!"

Charlie put Frankie's tank inside his backpack. "Mom, we're going."

Mama and Papa, reading at the kitchen table, waved at Charlie.

"Charlie, make sure to be home for lunch," said Mama.

"Stop by your grandparents' house on your way," said Papa. "They'll be happy to see you."

Charlie walked down the street to Grandma and Grandpa Chameleon's house. He knocked on the door and peeked in the windows, but nobody was home.

They must be out at the movies, Charlie thought.

Frankie blew bubbles inside the backpack as Charlie carried him to a nearby park with big trees, swings, and a merry-go-round. Right by the swings, Charlie saw two shadows. He squinted his eyes to block the bright sun. Someone with long ears towered over a figure cowering on the ground. Somebody was getting bullied!

"What do we do?" Frankie whispered. "Do we run away or do we help him?" Frankie peeked out of Charlie's backpack, shaking.

"We have to help him. I would want someone to help me," Charlie gulped.

Charlie gathered up his courage, ran toward the two shadows and shouted, "STOP! Leave him alone."

Right then, a big, bad, mean-looking bunny stood up, backed away from the other shadow, and stared at Charlie.

"Gulp. Oh, no. He's looking at us now," said Frankie, sloshing water out of the tank.

Charlie didn't back down. He looked into the mean bunny's eyes, trying his hardest to be brave.

"Or what?" the mean bunny yelled.

"Or . . . I'm gonna . . . I'm gonna . . . I'm gonna tell on you!" said Charlie.

"Ha, ha, ha! I don't care." The mean bunny laughed as he looked back at the figure shaking on the ground. "I'll finish this later," he sneered then turned away and thundered off.

"Whew! That was close. Thanks friend!" said the figure on the ground.

Friend? Charlie thought. He walked closer. The gecko brushed dirt off his knees, picked up his broken glasses, and put them on. Charlie hid a giggle. The gecko looked silly with lopsided, broken glasses.

"I'm Gary Gecko. What's your name?" Gary asked, with a nasal sounding voice.

"I'm Charlie. I'm new around here." As Charlie introduced himself, Frankie popped out of the backpack and waved a fin at their new friend. "He's new, too. His name's Frankie."

"It's nice to meet you. Thanks again for the rescue. I hate it when Boris corners me. He's always picking on me because I'm little and wear glasses."

"Boris?"

"Yeah, Boris Bunny, that's his name. You were brave to stand up to him."

"Well . . . it was scary. I would want help if someone bullied me."

"Hey, Charlie, you want to come to my house and play?" Gary asked.

Charlie and Frankie looked at each other and grinned. "Sure!" They walked through the park toward the houses.

Papa was right, Charlie thought. *If I take a chance, I might meet a friend.*

The three friends arrived at Gary's home. Charlie noticed it was only two blocks away from his new house. They were neighbors!

As they walked inside, Charlie saw a wrinkly gecko sitting on a couch wearing big glasses. She stared at the television.

Gary said, "Hi, Grandma."

"You're home early, Gary," said Grandma. "I see you brought a friend."

"Grandma, this is Charlie Chameleon. He just moved to New Town. He lives close, only a few blocks away."

"It's good to meet you, Charlie."

"Good to meet you too, ma'am."

"What wonderful manners you have, Charlie. You know, I met your Papa when he came to town last week. He is such a nice fellow," said Grandma. "Would you like to stay here for lunch? It's almost that time of day."

"Oh, wow, thanks, Grandma Gecko. I better call my mom and make sure it's okay."

Frankie poked his head out of the backpack tank. "What about me? Do you have meatballs for lunch? Maybe cheese?"

Grandma's mouth opened in surprise. "Merciful cats! What is that, a talking backpack?"

"No, Grandma. That's Frankie, Charlie's pet fish."

Charlie turned around so Grandma could see Frankie who smiled at Grandma, hoping for lunch.

"Well, I suppose I can find you some cheese, Frankie."

"Charlie, the phone is next to the front door. Go call your mama and ask if it's okay to eat with us," said Grandma.

Gary walked Charlie over to the phone and waited with him until Mama answered.

"Mama, can I stay for lunch with my new friend, Gary Gecko? His Grandma invited me." Charlie hoped Mama would say okay. He could smell lunch cooking. It smelled delicious.

"Charlie, Papa met Grandma Gecko when he looked at our new home. It's okay for you to have lunch with them. Make sure to say thank you."

"Okay, Mama, thanks."

"Charlie."

"Yes, Mama?"

"Please be home before dark."

The two friends walked upstairs to Gary's room. "Wow," Charlie and Frankie exclaimed. They saw stars, planets, telescopes, and model spaceships all around the room. "Your room looks so cool!"

"Yeah, it's a hobby of mine. I love outer space. My mom doesn't like it. She says it's too messy. The other kids make fun of me, but I don't care." Gary looked around his cluttered room. Charlie was already playing inside a model spaceship, pretending to fly in space.

Gary showed Charlie his stars and planets. They played spaceship for hours.

Charlie looked out the window and saw the sun setting. It was getting late. Mama would be worried.

"Oh, no! What time is it?" Charlie looked at Frankie snoozing in his portable tank. "Wake up, Frankie, we have to go. Thanks, Gary; I had a lot of fun."

Charlie grabbed his backpack with Frankie's portable fish tank, walked down the stairs, and rushed out the front door.

Gary waved goodbye to them from his bedroom window. "I'll see you tomorrow at school!"

Charlie ran home, excited about his new friend. He couldn't wait to tell everyone about Gary. He burst through the front door, just in time for dinner. The house smelled of pepperoni.

Charlie and Frankie took their places at the kitchen table.

Frankie stared at the pizza. He poked his head out of the fishbowl and said, "Pepperoni! Give me cheese, lots of cheese."

Ignoring Frankie, Mama looked at Charlie, sitting across from her at the table. "I was getting worried! Maybe it's time to get you a cell phone, Charlie. I'm glad you are home now. How did your day go?"

"It was great. We made a friend named Gary, and he has the coolest room!" Charlie picked up a piece of pizza, pulling off some pepperoni for Frankie. "I think I'm going to like New Town after all." Charlie slurped the cheese off the top of his pizza.

If only I didn't have to worry about that Boris Bunny.

Activity:

Cardboard Spaceship

- A large cardboard box, big enough for one or two children to sit in
- Scissors
- Glue or duct tape
- Markers
- Construction paper

Cut the top flaps off the box so there are two short cardboard rectangles and two long cardboard rectangles.

Fold two inches of the long side of the long cardboard rectangles down, then glue or tape those long rectangles to the long sides of the box on the small two inch flap. They should be about the same height on opposite sides. Give them time to dry. These are the wings.

They need to stay attached so they don't fall off while you are traveling through space.

Fold the last two inches of each end of the short cardboard rectangles down and then fold both the short cardboard rectangles in half. Fold them in the same direction, so the folds both point the same way.

Glue or tape the short cardboard rectangles to the front of the box, either side by side or perpendicular by pulling the two flaps you folded on the rectangle together then fastening them to the box. These are your nosecones/lights.

Decorate with construction paper cut-outs and markers.

Have a good flight!

Read more about it at http://www. ehow.com/how_4797441_spaceship-out-cardboard-box.html.

Charlie Starts a New School

RING! The alarm clock woke Charlie Chameleon and Frankie. Frankie jumped out of his fish tank and into his fishbowl while Charlie bounced out of bed. They looked at each other and rubbed their sleepy eyes.

They both remembered it was the big day and yelled, "School!"

Charlie rushed to his closet. He grabbed his backpack filled with new school supplies and Frankie's portable fish tank.

CRASH! Charlie bumped into a box on the hallway table. He ran downstairs, knocking over more boxes.

"Charlie!" yelled Mama Chameleon from the kitchen.

"Sorry, Mom!" Charlie yelled as he ran for the door with Frankie stowed away in his backpack fish tank.

"Wait a minute, please. You forgot your breakfast. Sit down and eat your Crispy Cricket Crunch cereal. You need protein in the morning."

SCREECH! Charlie came to a halt. "I forgot to eat." Charlie ate a few bites then stopped and stared out the kitchen window.

"What's wrong? Aren't you excited about the first day of school?" Frankie asked.

"I'm scared," Charlie whispered.

"Charlie," said Papa, standing behind his son, "would you like me to drive you to school?" Charlie nodded his head.

As they drove away from home, Charlie wondered why he was afraid to go to school. He was excited. He had a new backpack and his very own crayons, glue, scissors, and paper.

"Papa?" he asked, "Why am I so scared to go to school?"

"Well, you could be nervous because it's a new school." Papa looked at Charlie. "Why do you think you're scared?"

Charlie thought about this. *Why am I scared?* "I think I'm scared because I don't know anyone. Can you come with me?"

Papa laughed. "I can't go with you. You're a big chameleon now."

Charlie thought about Papa's answer. "You're right! I am a big chameleon now, and I have Frankie with me," he said. "But Papa, you will pick me up when school is over, right?"

"Of course I will. Now don't be late and make me proud!"

Charlie got out of the car and started to walk to the school.

"Hey, wait!" said Frankie from inside Charlie's backpack, still inside Papa's car. "Did you forget someone?"

"Oh, sorry, Frankie, I can't forget you. Bye, Papa. See you after school."

Charlie poked his head close to Frankie. "We're lucky, Frankie. Mama said the teacher will let you come to school with me."

Charlie stared at the front of the new school and slowly climbed up the steps. He walked down the long, empty hall to room number 38, his second grade classroom, and opened the door. A gray parrot with red tail feathers greeted him with a smile.

"You must be Charlie!"

"Yes, ma'am." Charlie was nervous. He could feel his skin tingling. Everyone was looking at him.

"I'm Mrs. Grey. Please take a seat anywhere. Class, this is Charlie, our new student," she announced to everyone.

Oh, no, Charlie thought. *They're going to see me change color and laugh.* Charlie took a deep breath and walked over to the first empty desk he saw and sat down. No one was laughing. Maybe he didn't change color after all.

Out of the corner of his eye, he saw someone waving at him. *What if someone's going to make fun of me?* thought Charlie.

He slowly looked over his shoulder. It was Gary Gecko, his new friend. He knew someone in his class. *This is good news!* Charlie thought.

He smiled and waved back. Everything was going to be okay.

He put Frankie, still inside the backpack, on the desk behind him and listened to his new teacher talk about math, his favorite subject.

This is easy! Charlie thought. He understood what was going on and already had one new friend in class. Charlie looked at Frankie, who was snoozing away in his fish tank. Math was not Frankie's favorite subject. He liked recess best.

After math, they practiced reading until the bell rang for recess.

Gary walked over to Charlie. "Hey, Charlie!"

"Hi, Gary! I'm glad we're in the same class."

"Want to play spaceships and astronauts together at recess?" Gary remembered how much fun he and Charlie had playing in the cardboard spaceship in his room.

"Sure! I don't know how to play, but you can teach me."

Gary and Charlie walked to the playground. Their classmates were playing in little groups.

Gary stopped and sat down under a tree. "Cool! No one ever wants to play spaceships and astronauts with me. They say it's not as much fun as playing tag."

Charlie sat down next to Gary. "I like learning new games," Charlie said.

From the school door, Mrs. Grey called Charlie's name. "Charlie, your fish needs to be out at recess with you. Come and get him, please."

"I'm coming, Mrs. Grey."

"Hey, Charlie. You brought your fish to school?"

"Yes, Frankie came with me. He loves recess better than almost anything. He was being nice when he met you at the park, but sometimes Frankie can be a little bossy. I'll be right back."

Charlie brought Frankie to the playground in his backpack tank. Frankie popped his head up and looked around. "You forgot me again!"

"Sorry, Frankie. I was so excited to go out I guess I did forget. What can I do to make you feel better?"

"Give me an extra meatball with dinner." Frankie spread his fins. "I want a meatball this big."

Gary stared at Frankie. "Your fish eats meatballs. That's so weird."

Frankie sucked in some air. "Charlie, your green friend here called me by the "W" word. I'm leaving." Frankie sank to the bottom of his fish tank.

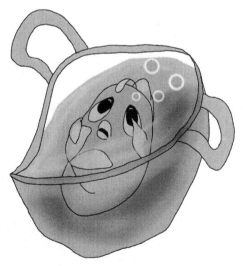

Charlie whispered to Gary, "Frankie doesn't like to be called 'weird.' It hurts his fish-feelings."

"Oh," whispered Gary. "I didn't know fish had feelings."

Gary poked his head into Charlie's backpack. "I'm sorry, Frankie. I won't say the "W" word again. I promise."

Frankie jumped up from the tank and gave Gary a big fishy-kiss, splashing water all over. "I forgive you, Gary Glasses. I'll take a nap now."

Gary was not happy. "Your fish has bad manners, Charlie. He called me Gary Glasses!"

Charlie took a deep breath. "Yes. I know. We're working on it. Can you teach me the game now?"

After playing spaceships and astronauts, the two friends, with Frankie in the backpack tank, walked together to get in line for lunch. Gary had packed his own lunch. They ate at a table, outside in the shade.

Charlie poked at his mystery meat lunch. It didn't look very good to him.

"Frankie, do you want some of my school lunch?"

Frankie looked it over. "No, thank you. I'll wait for my meatball at home."

"Want some of my lunch, Charlie? The lunches my mom makes taste a lot better than the school's lunches." Gary opened his lunch box.

Charlie peeked inside and saw baggies of ants and mealworms.

"Yuck!" said Frankie.

"Wait, there are crickets? My favorite! Would you like some, Charlie?"

"Sure! I didn't see them in the bag. I like crickets, too!" Charlie exclaimed, "Now I know

I should pack a lunch for school. Would you like some crickets, Frankie?"

"No," Frankie grumbled with his fins crossed, "I only want mealworm meatballs."

The bell rang again.

"Charlie, it's time to go back in. The afternoons are fun. We learn all about science!"

The students walked in a line to go back to class.

Charlie was happy with his new school, his new teacher, and his new friend. Everything was great except lunch. *Oh, well,* Charlie thought, *it could be worse.*

Before he knew it, the bell rang. Charlie looked at the clock. *It's 2:30 p.m. already? Time didn't fly so fast at my old school.*

"Bye, Charlie! I'll see you tomorrow!" Gary waved as he ran off.

"Bye, Gary!" Charlie said. Frankie waved goodbye, too.

Charlie looked at the street in front of the school. Papa was parked and waiting for him as promised. Charlie smiled and ran to the car. He got in to go home.

"How was your day, Charlie?"

"Great, Papa. My new friend, Gary, is in my class. We played together at recess."

"Charlie, that is good to hear. I talked to Mama. We think you can walk to school if you want to. What do you think? Are you feeling like a big chameleon?"

"Yes, Papa. Gary lives close to us, and he walks to school. Maybe we can walk to school together."

"Sounds like a good plan."

Papa parked the car and walked into the house with Charlie.

Frankie poked his head out of the backpack tank. "We are home. It's time for meatballs!"

"What is Frankie talking about, Charlie?" Papa wondered what Charlie's pet fish was up to this time.

"I promised Frankie I'd give him a meatball."

"Yes," said Frankie holding out his fins. "Make it this big."

"Did Frankie behave himself in school?"

"Yes, Papa, he was pretty good. I just had to make sure to bring him outside at recess. He took naps most of the day."

"Charlie," asked Mama, "do you have any homework?"

"There was no homework today. May I go upstairs and play in my room? My friend Gary taught me a new game. I want to play it with Frankie."

"Okay, Charlie. I'll call you down for dinner."

"Come on Frankie, I'll show you how to play spaceships and astronauts."

"Yes. Then I want meatballs, with lots of cheese."

Activity:

Frankie loves mealworm meatballs.

Here is a recipe for something you might like better, Chocolate Meatballs. (Adapted from tastebook.com/recipes/1308006-)

2 C. Granulated Sugar, 1/2 C. Milk, 1/2 C. Butter , 3 Tbs. Cocoa, 2 C. Oats, 1/2 C. Nut Butter, 1 tsp. Vanilla Extract. Mix sugar, milk, butter and cocoa in a large saucepan. Stir. Boil mixture for 3 minutes uncovered. Remove from heat and add remaining ingredients. Drop on a buttered cookie sheet. Let the "meatballs" cool completely, and eat.

Solution to the Encoded Message:

Dear Charlie,

    If you are reading this, that means you cracked the code. I hope you like your new home. Soccer won't be the same without you. I hope you find new friends and a soccer team in your new town. I can't wait to get a letter back from you. Write back to me using the same code. I miss you!

    Your friend,
        Tamika

Ellen Buikema is a writer, speaker and former teacher. A graduate of the University of Illinois at Chicago, she received her M.Ed. specializing in Early Childhood. She has extensive post-graduate studies in special education from Northeastern Illinois University.

Ellen writes short stories, poetry, adult nonfiction, and children's fiction, sprinkling humor everywhere possible. *Parenting . . . A Work in Progress,* her first book, is available worldwide. Find her at www.ellenbuikema.com, Twitter, LinkedIn, Facebook, and Google+.